For Joan,
who knew the deer and the dance
—M. L. R.

For Ursula,
who taught me to dance on my toes

And for M., R., & C.
—L. S.

BEACH LANE BOOKS
An imprint of Simon & Schuster Children's Publishing Division
1230 Avenue of the Americas, New York, New York 10020
Text copyright © 2014 by Mary Lyn Ray
Illustrations copyright © 2014 by Lauren Stringer
BEACH LANE BOOKS is a trademark of Simon & Schuster, Inc.
For information about special discounts for bulk purchases, please contact
Simon & Schuster Special Sales at 1-866-506-1949 or business@simonandschuster.com.
The Simon & Schuster Speakers Bureau can bring authors to your live event.
For more information or to book an event, contact the Simon & Schuster Speakers
Bureau at 1-866-248-3049 or visit our website at www.simonspeakers.com.
Book design by Lauren Rille
The text for this book is set in Aged.
The illustrations for this book are rendered in acrylic paint
on 140 lb Arches hot press watercolor paper.
Manufactured in China
0214 SCP
First Edition
10 9 8 7 6 5 4 3 2 1
Library of Congress Cataloging-in-Publication Data
Ray, Mary Lyn.
Deer dancer / Mary Lyn Ray ; illustrated by Lauren Stringer. – 1st ed.
p. cm.
Summary: A child who is in a woodland clearing to practice dancing spies
a deer and observes how it leaps and turns.
ISBN 978-1-4424-3421-9 (hardcover) – ISBN 978-1-4424-3422-6 (ebook)
[1. Deer—Fiction. 2. Dance—Fiction.] I. Stringer, Lauren, ill. II. Title.
PZ7.R210154Dee 2014
[E]—dc23
2012042214

Deer
Dancer

Mary Lyn Ray

Illustrated by
Lauren Stringer

Beach Lane Books
New York   London   Toronto   Sydney   New Delhi

There's a place I go that's green and grass,
a place I thought that no one knew—

until the day
a deer came.

When the deer saw me,
I stood so still,
I tried to be part of the grass.

I stayed still
as he came nearer, nearer
until he was so close
I could almost have touched him.

He looked at me. I looked at him.

Then he flashed his tail and leaped
back toward the trees where shadows
start and woods begin.

Did Nona somewhere meet the deer?
When she's teaching me to dance,
    she says,
    "Hold your head as if you're wearing antlers."

She says,
"Listen with your cheekbones."

"Look with the eyes in your shoulders."

But when she says
to reach like *this*,

or bend,

or spin,

I don't look like Nona.

So I come to practice in the place that's grass.

And the deer comes back.

He lowers his antlers
in greeting. I lower mine.

He starts to graze.

And I begin to feel a song
inside. Not one with words.
A song to dance.

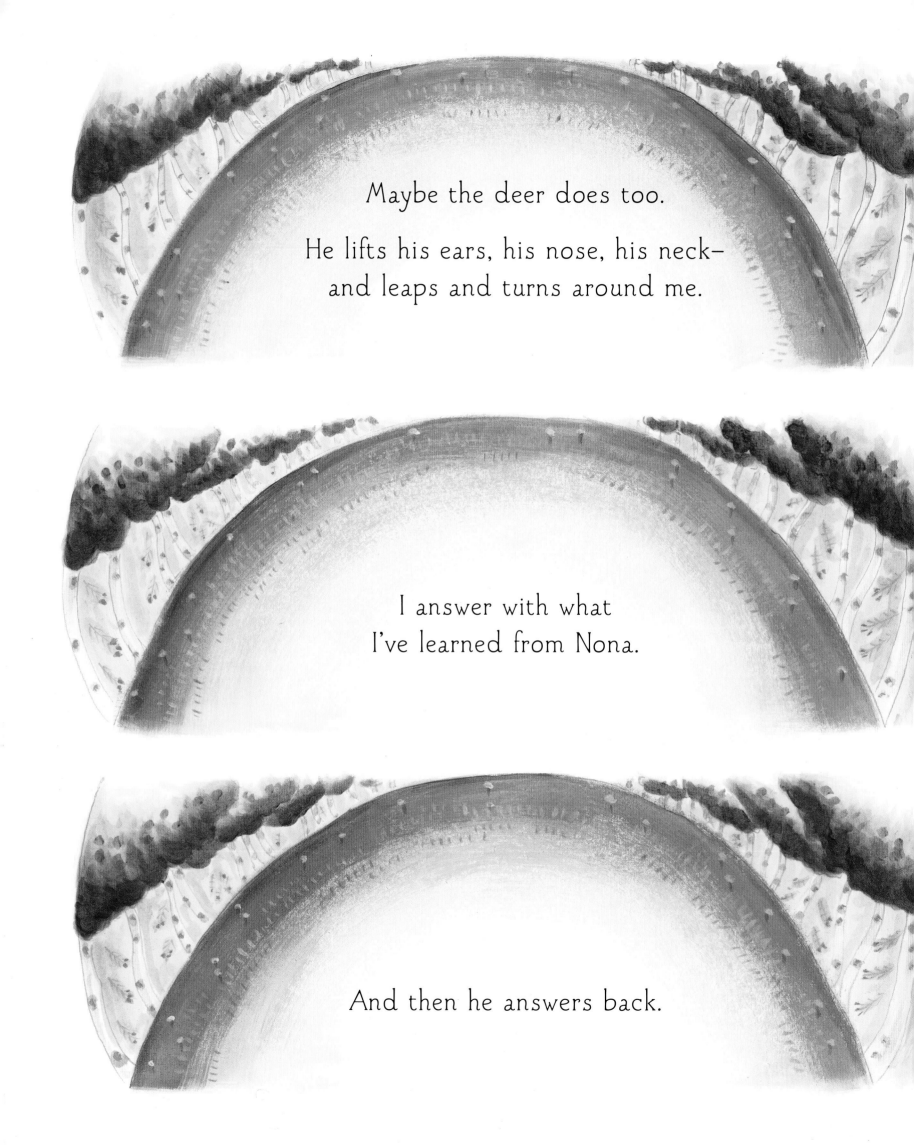

Maybe the deer does too.

He lifts his ears, his nose, his neck—
and leaps and turns around me.

I answer with what
I've learned from Nona.

And then he answers back.

He shows me how to leap
like him and leap like him—

throwing his antlers back.
So I throw mine, too.

And round and round we dance
a dance
for sun and green and grass—

until he turns again, and goes,

but leaves our dance
for me to dance.

I turn
the way that Nona says
our round earth
turns. I turn
the way my song
turns.

I leap.
I leap a hundred leaps.

And then *one more*.

I wish antlers were to keep.

But I have to go.

Now there's only empty grass.

Then shadows move
behind the trees.

I think the deer is back,
with other deer,
so they can dance
the dance deer dance—

when no one's there to see.